www.tredition.de

AF186349

Sven Frank

HUMAN MILK

© 2021 Sven Frank

Verlag und Druck:
tredition GmbH, Halenreie 40-44, 22359 Hamburg

ISBN
Paperback: 978-3-347-31783-3
Hardcover: 978-3-347-31784-0
e-Book: 978-3-347-31785-7

CHAPTER ONE

A white-ultra visible ambulance speed past like a space jet fluttering into the wreathed clouds. The city sleeps upon the northernmost point of Southampton Water, with an enviable confluence of water formed by the River Test and Itchen. Southampton is a city in England with uncommon features and awe-inspiring nature. Its splendid dense of greens stems from the impressive array of trees that can be found in the city.

Due to the immense development of the inner-city in Southampton, it has become a conducive home to the headquarters of both the Maritime and Coastguard Agency and the Marine Accident Investigation Branch. Most times, the city is the bassinet of an oceanic climate. Hence, its southerly, sheltered location enwraps it with enough warmth; which makes it one of the sunniest cities in the United Kingdom.

Inside the ambulance, a woman, who later in the hospital will be identified as Jennifer Jones, is gasping heavily for breath, a Paramedic Practitioner dressed in a grass-green outwear, covered from the neck to the waist with a Hi-Visibility, holds her feeble hand, Jennifer sleeps away into unconsciousness as the siren wail of the ambulance staggers decibels of crippling sound into reverberating echoes.

Monday, 12th of January, 2019, someone unknown was at the door. Jenny, as her friends fondly called her, meandered towards the door, oblivious of whoever hid behind her door awaiting her presence, called out to the person in a comely manner. There was no response; the silence was alarming.

Instead, the deep, husky grunts of double-crested cormorants silhouetted the silence that escaped the quiescence of the door. Jenny made a beeline for the door and unfastened it. Behind, a man- young, spectacled, heavily built, red lips, brown-pure white eyes, tall, straight to the core, with a curly black moustache, appeared in front of her, it was Jack; the man at the store the other day that helped her with $200.

"Life is all shitty, Jack" her parched lips opened up as she stretched her tiny legs into the gully full to the brim with clean and lucid water. The water oozed in rivulets as its trickling touches kept her body fecund with sensation.

She had walked him farther away from her threshold the moment she found out it was him knocking at the door. She had her reasons for everything that she does- she wanted to keep Jack out of sight, a bait to avoid the fury of her mistress.

At twelve, she lost her mum and dad. At twenty-one, she lost her maidenhood. She was molested by her Uncle until she summoned courage to flee his house. At twenty-four, she got a job to be a servant in the house of a proletariat. At thirty, she is with a man she admires, her libido heavy with the detritus of an amorous rollercoaster. Jennifer Jones is indifferent about the mystery of faith, hope, miracle and happiness; life has never been any good to her.

Her penetrative eyes unable to avoid Jack's red lips, her mind is full of diverse lascivious thoughts. Behind them, strangers slopped forward and backward, trying to meet up for their respective schedules.

"Jenny, I love you" Jack pressed his red lips upon hers, she stared motionlessly, there was no trembling, only flutters of butterflies, she couldn't believe her eyes. He wants her, too. The last time she fell in love, it was a boy that ran away with all the money she saved up. She sobbed for countless nights waiting for him to return, but he never returned. She had sworn never to embrace love.

"We had only met two days back at the store" Jenny pulled away as Jack tried to hold onto her tightly.

"Yeah, I know, this shouldn't be really hard, Jenny."

"I don't want to do this anymore. Life isn't a bed of roses."

"I found happiness the day I ran into you at the nearby store"

"I have lost so many battles trying to find joy, I love you and I do not want to lose you, too."

Jack couldn't believe what he had just heard, his heart skipped triple beats, his toes wrenched with cold. After she left, he trudged the road back to his cottage with those words curled into a knot inside his abs-ridden stomach.

That night, he found sleep unaffordable, he sat on the bed, strumming repeatedly his acoustic guitar.

******

Time sauntered past, Jenny couldn't believe all that was happening to her. She had fallen in love with a man whose affection and tenderness overwhelmed her. Last night, Jack had a full taste of her lips, he was totally irresistible, he fondled every part of her body; it felt like an ignition thrown into a wild-field doused with oil.

He promised to take away from the house she lived in; he promised to ferry her in his car to the Medieval City Walls; he promised to live his whole life for her comfort; he promised to get married to her before the celestial chariots of the heavens and earth. The future she keenly desired seem to be within her grip and she was ready to fight anyone to keep it.

In her dream, she wanders into a meadow, behind her is Jack, scurrying towards her with a handtied luxury red rose. Her grin settled subtly into the night's darkness every time she wakes up from such dreams. For the first time, she felt happiness and joy wring her intestines. Unfortunately, the best moment does not absolve longevity. Her nightmare began the day she wanted to make him a surprise Battenberg cake to announce to him the news of her pregnancy.

******

Jenny's cellphone blared out, after the fifth ring, she scrambled about trying to get hold of it, she rubbed her hands against the apron tied around her waist in a bid to remove the sticks of mixed flour glued to her fingers. She only thought of Jack as she began to speak to the caller.

"Hello… this cellphone belongs to an accident victim"

"Who…?" She didn't recognize the voice. Although, she knew it wasn't Jack.

"His ID card says his name is Jack. His car ran into the railing of Itchen bridge and tumbled" The unknown voice retorted.

She screamed. The cellphone fell out of her hands. She tried picking it up as she hurriedly dashed out of the house. The sky became grey and hazy to Jenny as she approached the scene of the accident. His body laid upon a stretcher, the Paramedic Practitioner pronounced him dead just as she ran towards his body. She paused. It was simply unbelievable. Tears dropped from her eyes, her mouth torn wide open, her world crumbled as those words sunk into her ear. Immediately, she fainted and fell to the ground.

****

At the hospital, Jennifer receives aides and regains consciousness. *What is the point of living*, she bites her lips with so much regret and sorrow. Jack is gone. She is too ashamed to return back to the house, there is a baby

9

in her womb, her life is slipping out of her grip, everything is sour, there is no place to call home; no woman to call mother; no man to call father; no Jack to call a heartthrob; no path for the broken soles of her life.

CHAPTER TWO

Silhouettes of two unidentified people lurk around the rear end of the ward, the wishy-washy lightbulb dangles inertly from a wire stuck to the plafond, Jenny is perturbed, unable to close her eyes. Her feeble body stays upturned towards the plafond of the room. The room is ordinarily phlegmatic, the walls are scrupulously spotless, the wind sits upon the windowsill, few inches farther from the body of her hospital cot; to her, the world seems vapid. She sobs again at the thought of Jack's death.

She moves her hands softly across the face of her belly, she thinks about her unborn child and his dead father. As a young lady who never enjoyed the fortune of being loved and catered for by her parent, the day the doctor told her she was up the duff, she vouched never to allow her children suffer the same fate.

Before the Doctor left, he told her the result of the amniocentesis carried on her. *Your baby is fine, Jenny.* He said before strolling out of the room. She mutters silently to herself 'I have just one reason to live'. The fate she suffered as a child, she was never going to allow her child suffer the same. The news of her baby's wellness shrug off some of the scurf of regret the demise of Jack enamored her mind with.

She thinks about his carcass; his red lips, heavily-built body, his curly black moustache and brown-pure white eyes. They are all gone, like the wisp of smoke. She read

11

some time ago in a book: *Death's Acre: Inside the Legendary Forensic Lab the Body Farm Where the Dead Do Tell Tales*, about the processes of human decomposition; she groans heavily as imaginative images of Jack's carcass slid through her mind. The fact that she is never going to see him again wrecked her totally.

****

Someone appears from the corridor that lead into the emergency ward, the figure struts through the hallway delicately, a lady for sure but her walk-carriage dazzled like that of a nurse. As she edges closer, styled with a white dress, fine-suited apron, her eyes glisten like sapphires, her cologne smells like roses drenched with coriander, when she gets to Jenny's cot.

"Hi, Jenny"

Jenny looks at her shabbily. She raises her head up to get a better glance at the face of the nurse even though the doctor warned her not to exert too much pressure on herself in order to aide her recuperating process.

"I am Sarah"

Jenny still doesn't answer. She is only interested in talking to anyone that would feed her ears with the miraculous news of Jack's resurrection from death. Unfortunately, there was no one.

"Can I be your friend?"

Jenny rubs her eyes, the words she just heard seem surreal. All her life, only Jack has openly requested to be her friend, she peers into Sarah's face, speechless and spellbound, Sarah sits close to her on the bed, she holds Jenny's hands and touch her face with so much interest evident in her facial disposition.

****

Sarah is extremely kind and amiable. She wittingly and carefully absorbs Jenny's grief, gifting her a hand of friendship, Jenny becomes glad again. Although, the spiraling bout of Jack's sudden death still keeps her fecund with sadness.

"Can I go see his body?" Jenny pleads, throbbing to behold the lifeless and cold state of her high-spirited lover. Sarah pretends to be distracted. Jenny yells out, *Can I go see his body?*

"I want to tell him his unborn child is fine"

Sarah is quiet. She thumps her left foot to the marbled floor like she is blown away by shame.

"I want to tell him the name of his child"

The doctor ambles in like a bolt from the blue. He moves closer to Jenny, as he instructs Sarah to help check another patient in the next ward. He is an ex-soldier according to what Sarah told Jenny, his arms are sturdy, big enough to intimidate a wrestler, he gently touches her tiny wrist then he pulls the stethoscope hung around his neck and put it to her chest, after a while, he hangs it back around his neck and speak to Jenny.

"You need to rest"

"I want to see Jack's body"

"No, you can't"

"Doc, I want to kiss his cheeks before he is buried" tears swell up in her eyes resembling the precedent of a cloudburst in the sky, her lips dense with flakes of misery, he doesn't look at her face for few minutes, the tears begin to drop like splattered raindrop, he reaffirms his stance and said.

"I am sorry you wouldn't be able see him"

Before he dawdles out of her sight, he turns. "Jack is going to be buried tomorrow" he divulges to her. Jenny looks at him, stupefied and damaged to the point of irrationality, she runs out of her hospital cot and grab the double-chested suit of the doctor, she squeezes his blue-red rectangular strip shirt, her voice broken and futile in its attempt at vocalization

"Jack…"

There is a bit of silence before she continues.

"Take me to him, Doc"

"He is gone to rest, Jenny" he holds her frail arms, his fingers tighten the sleeve of her garment that reeks of dust and loneliness, he pulls her away from his body to her cot gently, she lay quietly, unaware of the presence of the Doctor anymore, he covers her body with the cot's soft duvet made from the plumes of different birds, and walks away as far as the shrilling noise of her caterwaul couldn't reach.

Today, Jack is buried and Jenny is in her cot begging God for his return, his kisses and caresses; she wants him back.

Tuesday, 25th of January, 2019, it is the fourth day after Jack's funeral. The light from the sun pervading Jenny's naked body is luminous in its dazzling rays of multiplicity, Jenny is prepared to visit Jack's tomb after Sarah succumbed to her endless pleads. As she wears her gown, diverse emotions run through her spine, she is happy, she is sad; she is a portrait of headless headlamps.

In few minutes, Sarah strolls in, her head shimmering with droplets of rainfall, there is a wet umbrella in her hands, her heels tiny at the lower end of their throttle, they move quietly out of the ward into the hallway, the rain keeps drizzling, Sarah unlatches the umbrella up to the sky as they leap into the hospital's uncovered veranda.

****

"This is where he is buried" Sarah points to a tomb with letters and dates inscribed on the body. There is a wet rose flower atop the tomb, there is another tomb equally opposite to Jack's tomb, but the letters inscribed on it says it belongs to a lady. Jenny is too weak to begin another wailing.

I hope to live with you in paradise, she consoles herself timidly. She bends and places the roses given to her by Sarah on his tomb, she whispers under breath, she holds the granite stones on his tomb, she selects one and hides it in her purse. *I'm going to have this punctured and made to hold a necklace for my child,* she tells Sarah this as they leave for the hospital.

****

Jenny searches the house for bracelet Jack gave her. She doesn't find it. *I want to give my baby,* she mutters to herself as her fingers scurries through the stockpile of abandoned papers in her caisson. She still doesn't find it. She stops and turn around to peer into the mirror hung to the ridgepole of her room's wall. The thought of her baby peeks into her mind slightly, happiness blossoms in her heart every time she remembers that Jack's baby lives in her small tummy. She promises herself to give the best life to her baby. The sun blazoned into darkness. It is bed time call for Jenny.

The scrunch of a mouse wakes Jenny up from sleep, the dog next door is barking into the empty and dark-ridden city, the night is unusually longer, Jenny tries gathering her body out of the bed, something seems unpleasant and weird, her child. Her mind is unsettled, she places her hands carefully on her belly, nothing is moving, there is no kick or jostle, she is scared to the innermost innards of her mind, she picks up her cellphone and request for an ambulance.

In a jiffy, the ambulance arrives, the city is dark, a paramedic practitioner walks her out of her house into the ambulance, she gets laid on a stretcher as the ambulance galloped into the dark road of Southampton.

After series of examination conducted on Jenny, the doctor finds out that her child is dead. He reluctantly spills the news to Jenny,

"Doc, what is wrong?"

"Your baby"

"What is it about my baby"

"Your baby is dead, Jenny"

This time around, she didn't faint, she stands up from her cot and walk out of the ward calling Jack's name repeatedly like an insane woman, the doctor runs after her.

CHAPTER THREE

Jenny's flippant drive towards the extrinsic chassis of the hospital drew the undivided attention of many lurking around. Sarah darts after her. Sarah's ferocious outcry enshrouds the cosmos of the hospital with fear and trembling. Jenny does not look back; her body benumbed to the livingness of the earth; her heel pallid, her face feverish enough to apprise anyone of her predicament.

Before she sauntered into the road, Sarah gets to her, Jenny startled like a boy caught in the act of theft by his mom, tears slide out of her eyes, her lips remake the morning brume with murmurs as Sarah grasps her arm. Jenny looks away. *You'll be fine, Jenny*. Sarah rejoins. This was the same thing Sarah told her the day Jack died, she had promised to be her fulcrum. Yes, she was but Sarah never told her that her child would have to be delivered dead.

She hates it that Sarah is here again to console her. Sarah holds on tight to her, not allowing her slip away from her grip, Jenny gave a nebulous snort as she lay down her downtrodden and sullen face on Sarah's white garment

"Jack's child is gone" she yells out to Sarah.

"Be thankful you are alive, Jenny" Sarah consoles as she snappily walks her back into the building.

"I have nothing to live for anymore"

"No, you have to live for yourself, Jenny"

Jenny's hope has been dashed after the doctor informed her that the child in her belly is dead. All of her body developed a sudden disdain for life and its continuity. No one in the world is capable of salvaging a vineyard of joy for her. She keeps the voices swiveling in her head to herself, she doesn't spill anything to her- Sarah.

Sarah accompanies back to her cot, her hands swaddled around Jenny's slender waist, Jenny doesn't act like she has a plan B. After she successfully walks Jenny back her ward, Sarah leaves for the doctor's office, as she darts towards his office, she stumbles upon the doctor at the threshold of his office, he is with a man, the director of a company that is into the production of nutrition products. Sarah recognizes his face; she has seen him at the hospital on several occasions she can't seem to remember, hastily she speaks.

"Jenny is back in, Doc"

"Alright, I'll join in a jiffy" He snaps back as he surreptitiously leads the man away through the hallway.

****

Jenny quietly succumbs to the instructions of the doctor. *I'm going to end my life after I deliver my baby, I'll live together with them- Jack and her baby, in paradise,* she mutters to herself.

The room is dark, the windowsill drapes undulate in semblance with the directive of the whirlwind, her cot is weirdly hard tonight, since the doctor left, Sarah didn't return to check her up, she mischievously assumes Sarah has returned back to her home, she quietly unties her scarf, she stands on top of the bed as she wrings the scarf in her hands tightly. The sound of a forthcoming individual sends her back into withdrawal, although it was the haggardly missteps of a man trolling the fence of the hospital back to wherever he was going to.

This time around, nothing is going to stop her. She summons herself out of the bed again. This time she reaches out elegantly to knot around the neck of the fan her loosed scarf. All she plans to do is tie that same knot around her neck and fall away from the top of her bed so she can get strangulated. Unfortunately, at the verge of knotting the scarf-tied-to-the-fan around her neck, Sarah barged in unprecedented and stopped her from proceeding in this depressive-provoked and insane act.

****

"Jenny, you can't keep hurting yourself like this" Sarah turns around to switch on the room's lightbulb. "How on earth did you do that with no light in here?" Sarah adds. Jenny is quiet, *why did Sarah have to show up again*, her mind is cluttered with unvoiced questions, these questions occupy the silence she nestled when faced with questions she feels deserve no answers.

"I love you, Jenny" Sarah joins "Please, your life can still be very beautiful"

Jenny sees all of this as mere repetition of what Sarah did the first time. "What if Sarah dies?" she rejoins in her mind "Who is going to save me?" The last time Sarah wheedled her, she lost Jack's baby; now Sarah is here, cajoling her out of brooding and suicide, what is going to happen afterwards, another pandemonium? She mumbles to herself.

Sarah sleeps together with her on the cot. She narrates to her diverse stories although the one that proved to be the lock to Jenny's puzzle is the story about a woman who survived cancer. The next day, Jenny gets to be transferred to a psychiatric ward as instructed by the doctor. Sarah had told him everything that transpired the other night.

****

Sarah comes around every day to see how Jenny is doing in her new ward; she spends ample time with her before she takes her leave. Jenny has become so comfortable around Sarah that she actually can't hide anything about her life from Sarah- she knows it all. Jenny's bra gets soaked from lactation as she has been unable to feed them to any child, while she wipes off the stain from her red-roses sleeveless top, Sarah hops in like a girl waving at her crush,

"Oh Jenny, what are you cleaning?"

"My nipples" Jenny replies embarrassingly, she has never had to disclose anything about her feminine body parts to other people, even when the doctor told her he was to deliver her of her dead child, she grumbled in her soul.

"Why?" Sarah inquires because the psychosis Jenny suffered some days back has made thoughts of Jenny, being a pregnant woman five days ago, elude her. Within few seconds, her mind is back to appropriateness, she becomes aware of the reason for Jenny's lactation,

"Oh, I remember now!"

Jenny gives a smirk as she lay her buttocks softly on the cot, while asking Sarah to come over and join her there.

"Can I discuss something with you" Sarah begs. The aura of their conversation changed immediately Sarah said this. Jenny curls her legs inward over the bed, she does this in a way that heralds into the mind the sitting posture of babies anticipating the hands of their mommas.

"Yes, you can" Jenny dispels this sudden sacredness with a comely remark.

"OK. There is a baby that lost its mother immediately it was given birth to"

"Ouch. That hurts" Jenny's eyes are quick to tears.

"This baby needs your help" Sarah continues "This baby needs milk, your milk"

"How is that going to work, Sarah?" Jenny peers into Sarah's glossy face like the answers were plastered on it.

Sarah plummets her hands into Jenny's small hands, *will you help this baby?*

This is so difficult for Jenny. She doesn't say anything after Sarah's question. She stands up, turns around to have a view of Southampton's sky filled with cormorants, she crackles her fingers one after the day as she ruminates on Sarah's request.

"You'll get paid. The baby is from a wealthy home and they are ready to feed and house you" She concludes.

"Ermmmhhhhhh" Jenny's mind is totally not convinced about doing this. She is only more concerned about the benefits she was going to derive from this bargain. She decides to do it in her sheer state of resignation rather than conviction.

CHAPTER FOUR

"We need to make sure that the raw materials are supplied as and when due in order to avoid any delay in production; this will improve delivery" a man in a double breasted black-grey suit vents out grudgingly to another man whose glaring distinctiveness is the color of his suit-navy.

The other man agrees to the recommendation of the man clothed in a black-grey suit, *we need to work on that as fast as possible,* he retorts.

"Yesterday, a customer complained heavily about the delay in delivery" He painfully narrates to the man in a double breasted black-grey suit. "I was totally stunned and speechless. I couldn't even utter a word to him" he adds as he inserts his right hand into his tiny trouser pocket.

It is a bright Monday morning, it is business as usual in the city, all issues need to be talked out as quick as possible in order to prevent a low outpour at the end of the week. Last week, there was a low turnout as delivery was delayed due to the unavailability of raw materials, the outcries and complaints of the customers had gotten to the doorstep of these two businessmen and they needed to find a solution to that.

While their discussion ensued, another customer- a short, obese woman, walked up to them with a pallid face, disgruntled and unhappy,

"Good morning" she says.

"Good morning, Madam" the man in navy suit is quick to respond, the other man adds wittingly, *what can we do for you?*

"My products were delayed, I didn't get them at the agreed time" she continues, *I can't keep up with this all the time, there is a marginal reduction in sales every time there is a delayed delivery.*

Her face remains stern as the man in a double breasted black-grey suit assures her that the issue will be resolved as the institution is making necessary arrangements to ensure that delayed delivery is avoided. As the woman quietly walks away from the two men, the man in a navy suit tells the other man that there are progressive plans on ground to recruit more HMPs to solve this problem, they heartily exchange handshake and depart.

****

This ward is unlike the other wards Jenny ever stayed in. The luxurious setting of this place absorbs her gaze so much that she incessantly peers at every item aesthetically arranged in the ward. She is glad, although this glee is bed-rocked by numerous questions. She loves the newness that this is going to herald to her; the comfort, sanity and peace of mind.

Every day, she is provided with extremely rich organic foods that are majorly consumed by the society's proletariat. The last time she ate a highly rich organic food was when Jack invited her over to his crib for a date, she ate and ate till she had no might to lift herself off the couch.

Last night, before she went to bed, after dinner, she found it uncanny, unbelievable and inexplicable that she is having all of this comfort to herself. She thought about Jack; his fatal fervor for their mutual love; his death that left her helpless and hopeless; the sudden death of their unborn child that wrecked her sanity. Now, she is in an exotic ward treated like a queen with meals that she could never afford.

As the days pass by, she regains her sanity as she is fortified by this stockpile of comfort and care. She becomes strong again. Sarah hasn't come to visit her. She misses Sarah because of the exciting conversation they shared when they are together; these conversations have consecutively saved her from being a suicide addict.

Most times, Jenny is confounded by the benefits she gets to enjoy by feeding her breastmilk to an unknown baby; this looks unbelievable but she promises herself to enjoy it while it last. Jenny has never seen the baby. Because of confidentiality, she is never allowed to see the baby. The presence and supply of all these luxurious benefits leaves her unbothered by the confidentiality of this agreement.

Wednesday, 2nd of March, 2019, somebody unusual is at the door knocking lightly, Jenny makes a beeline turn towards the door, although she was expecting no one. The sight of an old woman, grey-colored hair, curled to a smaller pose by the rage of senility, her eyes, deepened by the length of years she has spent on earth, she walks in majestically as Jenny stood glued to the other side of the door.

"Good morning, Jenny" her voice is a little bit shaky and at an equal proportion: uptight.

Hastily, Jenny retorts, *Good morning, Madam.*

I don't know you, Madam, Jenny opens up as she returns back into the room.

Jenny is slightly perturbed by the unprecedented appearance of this woman whom she has never seen before. It is quite easy in England to decipher the social stratification of a visitor through some striking features. These features- her coat, bag, heels, skin color, suggest that this woman belongs to the upper echelon of the English society.

"I am the grandma of the baby you indirectly breastfeed" the woman confidently reveals herself to Jenny.

"Oh, I'm really sorry" Jenny rushes to give her a warm hug, she continues, *you look so pretty.*

"That is so sweet of you, Jenny" Jenny presses her body closer as she inhales happily the alluring scent of her lavender.

Jenny is so glad that she didn't know when she started revealing all about herself to the woman. Impressively, at every statement that Jenny says, the woman chuckles, sighs, nods and gives her an undivided attention.

All of a sudden, she hands a cheque note of five thousand pounds to Jenny. Jenny is surprise, she doesn't know why she gave her this so she asks,

"Why are you giving me this"

"This is a token of appreciation from our family to you"

Before Jenny could say anything further, the woman throws a question to her suddenly,

"Would you love to continue breastfeeding our baby for another three months?"

Jenny is speechless and dumbfounded. The woman continues, *take your time to think about this properly, Jenny.* She places her hand softly over Jenny's shoulder.

"You will be moved away from this ward to a special sanatorium in Cornwall where you will be treated better than you are now," she concludes, "if you agree to this"

"Madam, urghhhhhhh"

"Take your time, Jenny" The woman gives her another comely hug and walks out of the ward.

****

"Do you think this is a great deal? Jenny confronts Sarah with this question. She has a huge confidence in whatever Sarah tells her to do. The only person on earth she confidently knows truly loves her is Sarah.

Sarah came around a day after the woman had visited Jenny with a mouthwatering cheque of five thousand pounds.

"I think this is a great offer" Sarah peers into Jenny's innocuous face, "your life is going to become better"

"Is this a yes from you, Sarah?" Jenny mumbles to her.

"Yes, it is, baby girl" Sarah confidently adds, "go ahead"

Jenny agrees.

CHAPTER FIVE

Southampton is 151 miles away from Cornwall. The idyllic tingle of estuaries, the frosty whiff of sandy beaches, the exciting exhibit of small rocky coves and headlands, are the sheer modulation of the city's existence. The fringes of the city 's quiescence. Egrets spread their shrieks over the rooftop of the buildings flanked by huge palm trees.

Jenny has been moved away from the luxury-ward where she stayed several days feeding indirectly an unidentified baby. All of these is happening because Sarah gives her a go ahead. Jenny's new gown is dench; Sarah had purchased it for her prior to the day she was supposed to leave for the sanatorium.

Over the past weeks, Jenny has totally transformed into a lovely young lady. She is unbothered about what the future holds. At the moment, she is happy, beautiful and hopeful. As long as she keeps giving out her breast-milk to the unidentified baby whose mother had died as she heard, all of this excitement and convenience was not hitting a hiatus soon.

Jenny is paid $5000 per month to consistently give her breastmilk to this baby as agreed with the madam that visited her at the luxury ward. To her utmost surprise, she is supplied with quality organic food, massage, cosmetic treatments and entertaining events that make her lively and happy again.

The sanatorium is spacious, strikingly different from the hospital. Few people trooped in and out of the sanatorium. Every time she thinks about this, the aesthetic outlining of the sanatorium and its downright serenity clouds her thoughts again. The women in here are extremely beautiful; she doesn't know why they are here, she can only speak for herself, but she finds them utterly attractive.

They look like benign angels sent from the pinnacle of the heavens down to the earth. Most times, she finds herself struggling with an irrepressible urge to start a conversation with one of them. Although, she has been unable to do that successfully. The last time she tried, the lady, appealing and radiant, got called by unknown man into a room with a golden doorknob.

****

Today, Jenny sets out to accomplish this task: 'Hello, I am Jenny', the lady close to the ceramic wall festooned by a small vase of rose flowers looks up at Jenny, her eyes twinkle like falling stars.

'Hi, I am Charlotte' she retorts extending her right hand towards Jenny for a brief handshake. Jenny does not hesitate to wreathe her hand into Charlotte's comely hand.

'You got here some days back, right?' Charlotte unashamedly asks. She looks older than Jenny, there is a knife-cut scar around her wrist, her face is unlike Sarah's face, but her gesture isn't different from Sarah's.

'Yes, I got here some days back' Jenny glares at Charlotte, overwhelmed by the smoothness of her red skin. She could not spot any blister on Charlotte's face.

'Follow me' Charlotte adds, 'I will introduce you to my friend, Amber'

On their way towards the end of the lobby, Jenny talks about her life, Charlotte sympathize with her. She tells her about her best friend, Sarah, the lady whom she owes her existence to.

'What an angel Sarah is to you' Charlotte brushes aside her braid, before she could continue, Jenny asks,

'How long have you been here?'

Hurriedly, Charlotte replies, 'We have been here for five years!'

'We?!' Jenny is confused, 'What do you mean by 'we'?'

'Yes, I mean I and Amber'

'Great!'

****

Amber darts forward, although Jenny does not recognize her until Charlotte's chin widens into a desirable and alluring smile,

'Oh, is that Amber?' Jenny asks as she turns to peer at her again, but before she could complete the turnaround, Amber already got into Charlotte's wide arms like a toddler.

Amber is shorter, completely unbothered by Jenny's intimidating gaze. While Jenny lurks around, covertly provoked to think about her favorite moments with Sarah by these two beautiful beings, Charlotte introduces Amber to her,

'Jenny, this is Amber' Charlotte does not stop, 'I found her when I got to this sanatorium'. There is something endearing about these two that Jenny finds appealing, before Jenny is totally caught in these fleeting thoughts, Charlotte introduces her to Amber,

'This is Jenny, Amber' they do not exchange handshake like Charlotte initially did with Jenny, but Amber thrusts towards her and strokes her bright cheeks with her hands, Jenny grins.

****

Jenny has found so much peace and joy in the company of these two lovely beings. She does not miss Sarah as much as she did in the first week. She is happier and comfortable now. Her room is two rooms away from Charlotte's room, but Amber's room is not anywhere close to hers. At morn, they meet up for exciting discussions and jokes. They talk about live; the events that spool into it unexpectedly; the grief that everyone, silently, embody; the joy that they seek in the presence of loved ones that have died.

Last night, Jenny asked Charlotte and Amber if they had any plans to leave the sanatorium after spending another two or three years here, they seemed uninterested and evasive as none gave her an expressive response. She was bothered about this apathetic display from her friends, she decided to ask again when they meet the next day for their daily exercise.

Jenny could not wait to meet up with her friends after an entirely sleepless night. They meet up at the spa at 10:00am. Charlotte kisses both Jenny and Amber on the cheek. They have become quite inseparable during the day, only at night will you find them separated. Jenny is not pleased by the gestural responses of her friends when she asked if they had any plans to leave last night, she takes the bait again as they sauntered into the doorway.

Jenny plunges forward, and turns backward. Charlotte and Amber stand befuddled by this unusual act, Charlotte is perturbed, Amber speaks up,

'Is anything wrong, Jenny?'

'Yes'

'What is it?' Charlotte interrupts, as she edges closer to the Jenny.

'Do you have any plans to leave this sanatorium?' Jenny speaks up loud and clear.

Charlotte and Amber chuckles and walk past her. They utter no words to her. Jenny is ashamed. She feels avoided and unwanted so returns back to her room pondering about pathetic display from her friends again,

'What could be wrong with these ladies?' she asks herself as she sleeps off.

CHAPTER SIX

A few months later, Jenny's breasts were not producing milk in a surplus proportion anymore, she was producing a lesser quantity of milk; which was of little addition to the amount of milk needed at the Sanatorium. Jenny is worried; she ponders over the thought of her leaving the Sanatorium anytime soon; she thinks about Amber and Charlotte; her two close friends whom she met here; she thinks about her finances and how hard she was going to find it surviving on the street of England with no stable source of income.

The only valuable thing left in her life perhaps she ends up leaving the Sanatorium is Sarah; her first friend whom she has not seen since she got transferred to the Sanatorium. 'I will go over to Sarah; she is going to let me stay at her home while I pervade the street of England for a job,' Jenny tells herself, unbeknown about the covert plan of the institution to make her fertile with breast-milk again. She thinks about telling Charlotte and Amber about this; she gags her mind with brooding. After so much brooding, she chose to tell them later in the week.

The doctor comes in while Jenny lay quietly on her bed, she is worried about this unusual visit from the doctor, the doctor has never been to her room prior to this unprecedented visit, 'he is sure around to ask to me to leave the Sanatorium very soon' she mutters indignantly to herself. Her mind is purged by trepidation at the sight of the doctor. 'Hello, Jenny' he continues, 'how are you doing today?'. She unhesitatingly retorts, 'I am fine, Doctor'

They stare at each other in ways that seem suspicious, although Charlotte and Amber once told her that the doctor did have a weird look and this isn't intentional as he has proven over the years that he is a wonderful and cheerful being, so Jenny shrugs off the thoughts of his visit covertly implying that she is leaving the Sanatorium anytime soon.

'I got to know that you have been producing a lesser quantity of breastmilk' his voice is bland, empty of any ulterior motive, Jenny is fixated to the ordinariness of his diminutive stature, he snaps her back to life with a terse question, 'are you here, Jenny?'

'Yes, I am' she pleads, 'sorry about that', he stretches his hands forward and gives her a drug, Domperidone (Motilium); he explains intelligently, 'This is a drug to increase the quantity of breastmilk your breasts will produce,' he adds, 'ensure you do not brood over this as it is common amongst breastfeeding mothers'. Jenny smiles sheepishly, 'thank you so much, Doctor' she says as she unfolds the drug inquisitively at the presence of the doctor who was about taking his leave.

****

'I think it is natural that my breastmilk reduces as it is over some months since my unborn baby died tragically,' Jenny tells Charlotte, 'I think the drugs issued out to me by the doctor will only help to preserve the breastmilk for a little while'. Charlotte chuckles, Amber climbs over the chair like a child folding his legs upon a swing, 'I think my time is up here' Jenny is still embattled. 'Do not worry about it, Jenny' Charlotte speaks up, 'We have been here for so long now and there is way to go about it', there is surprised look on Jenny's face, 'what do you mean, Charlotte?'

Amber peers into her eyes and says, 'Yes, Jenny. There is a more natural and attractive way to get your breastmilk back,' she relaxes her back properly over the chair as she said that. Jenny is confused about these statements made by her friends. 'What do they mean?' she plunges her face forward into the air, wondering what her friends meant by uttering those statements. This mystery beclouds Jenny's mind with utter haziness.

She looks around, Charlotte and Amber chitchat, unbothered by Jenny's disturbed look, she looks at them again, she suspects something unusual about the ambience of the Sanatorium. Ever since she asked Charlotte and Amber about leaving the Sanatorium anytime soon, their lethargic and apathetic disposition towards her has left her wondering if everything was appropriate about this Sanatorium,

The pregnant women around became more evident and suspicious to her. She wonders why they are here; whom pregnancy do they carry; what happens to the baby after they are delivered by these mothers; why are the breastmilk from these mothers given to another baby; she is helpless as not even Sarah would beckon to unbind this ambiguity taming her mind.

Charlotte notices this weird lavender oozing out of Jenny's face, 'I know you are worried, right?'

'Yes, I am' Jenny innocently grips her hands, behind her, another pregnant woman lay on a green-white couch, her face, upturned towards the ceiling, beside this woman, Amber is talking to an unidentified woman, the woman speaks like a girl that has just found love.

Charlotte continues, 'What I meant to say the other time is that you will have to become pregnant again'. Jenny is startled by these words, she is speechless, trying to speak seem like pulling a truck with her tiny brawl. Charlotte adds, 'Our lives became better when we got in here', another woman clothed in velvety gown appears from the hallway down the end of the room. 'What do you mean by saying I should become pregnant again?' Jenny's voice hurts with so much fatigue and furiousness, 'For who? How? Is that the natural and most attractive method to get my breastmilk back?' Jenny is restless, everything seems to crushing before her very own eyes.

'You have to do this if you do not want to return to your old life, Jenny' Charlotte gets up and shudders her way into Jenny's face, 'Listen to me. You have to give all it takes to survive and stay healthy. Do you want to return to your old life? A life bereft of joy, wealth, organic food and friends.' At this point, Jenny could not help herself from weeping, her lips warble as she tried speaking but there was nothing she could say.

'This is a rare opportunity, Jenny. The lives we got now is a result of all that has been bestowed upon us in this Sanatorium. I and Amber are eternally grateful for this rare privilege to become good humans again.' Charlotte remarks heartily.

****

Two days later, Jenny finds herself in the Doctor's office, she couldn't tell what the Doctor wants her to do, but she knows it is about her inability to produce the same quantity of breastmilk again since he was at her room some days back to give her a drug for improvement.

'Good day, Jenny'

'Hello, Doc'

'I know you are worried. This is not new here'

'What do you mean, Doc?'

'Charlotte did tell you about becoming pregnant again. That is the only natural and conducive way to get your breastmilk back.'

'Doc…'

'Jenny, you are going get paid. A sum bigger than what you receive now for feeding the baby'

'What do I need to do now?'

'Become a surrogate mother!'

He adds, 'You will be given 50,000 pounds and your stay in the Sanatorium will be extended'.

CHAPTER SEVEN

The weather is cold. Light snow begun falling the previous night. It is the same weather condition this morning. An unknown man walks across the snowgrass towards the alley that leads to the office of the Director. He wears a crisp smile as he moves closer to the office of the Director. His movement is suspicious, he walks carefully like it is his first time in the Sanatorium, he looks tactless, although he leverages on his confidential pose which beclouds every strain of anxiety and confusion on his face.

The Sanatorium is quiet and frosty, the leaves bristle with a subtle thirst for warmth, but the sun is without its power; the cold is riveting, only for a justified reason will anyone choose to enter this snowfall. Jenny and her friends- Charlotte and Amber are locked within the walls of their rooms, curled sheepishly around a thick duvet. The unknown man holds a leather bag, he does not seem like a criminal because of his modest dressing fully adorned by a jacket to keep him warm. He ruffles his hair softly, snows drop upon his shoes in small flakes, he seems to be here to meet the Director.

Numerous persons have been here to see the Director for covertly discussed business transaction. Everyone except Jenny knows that the liquid gold is the main reason for this usual appearances from strangers. Jenny does not know about this, she is still bothered about the natural way of recovering her breastmilk which means that an unknown guy will get her pregnant. Before the man walks farther close to the Director's office as described to him by the google map, he brings out his smart phone and dials the number of the Director,

'Hello, Director'

'Howdy?'

'Fine. I am here, already'

'Oops, I will be with you soon'

In the blink of an eye, the Director strolls out ebulliently, they both exchange pleasantries like business partners do every time they meet to do business. They seem to have met several times prior to this particular meeting, but they never met in the past for any business engagement. They had much to speak as it did not take long before the discussion set rolling. The unknown man, Thomas William, who decided to feign as an unidentified businessman, is here to find out about the activities carried out in the Sanatorium. The Director is unaware of this, he starts out quick to convince him of the potentialities of the liquid gold and the institution.

****

'Do you want to check around?' The director is wittingly clever in deploying this routine as a bait to impress every new customer. It has been widely purported that the Sanatorium has a pulchritudinous structure, coupled with a flowery landscape tranquil and fascinating. Williams jerks excitingly, feigning to be a businessman interestingly interested in the institution,

'I will love to do that'

While they move, they laugh intermittently about the funny cum weird sounds that oozed out of their shoes as they unrepentantly crunch a snow. 'Wow, it is a beautiful sight to behold!' The unknown man expresses emphatically, 'Totally beautiful, I am impressed.' The Director blushes, his cheeks become red like a baby leaping to hug his returning mother, 'The liquid gold is more precious and special'. He continues, 'We got an impressive amount of raw materials supplied over the week,' he unhesitatingly engages the new customer about the benefits of the liquid gold,

'What is a liquid gold?' he ponders about the term: liquid gold, he is braced by zest to know what it is about and what value does its accumulation herald.

The Director boldly speaks up, 'The liquid gold is used to produce diary products', he adds, 'the liquid gold contains properties that help infants sleep well at night; this also protects the baby. The liquid gold is quite good for the environment; it is also an energy booster; it is a natural energy booster; it helps to build up the body muscles; it contains natural compounds that can build up the muscles; it is also a fast route to gain more weight if consumed; it helps in dealing appropriately with acnes; it helps to cure sore throat; it can be used to fight E. Coli;

it can be used to fight Crohn's disease; it is helpful against diabetes; it can be used to treat Arthritis; finally, there is a possibility it can be utilized to fight cancer.'

The Director stops for a moment and asks, 'Sir, what do you think about it?'

It is utterly impossible to turn a deaf ear to the vital and pertinent components of this liquid gold, the new customer is extremely stunned and speechless, he stammers as the Director asked the question, 'Www-woowww… This totally swept me off my feet', he keeps acting like he was here for an innocuous purpose. The Director smiles gullibly, he feels he has just unlocked the loyalty of a new customer; which means that his bait has been effective. 'Is there a business now?', the Director proceeds to ask, 'Yes, I want this', the Williams replies instantaneously.

Quietly they leave with both parties feeling excited and enthusiastic about the trajectory of this impressive business agreement.

＊＊＊＊＊＊＊＊＊＊＊＊＊＊

Williams could not stop thinking about the liquid gold. How possible is a single thing able to do all that this liquid gold can do? The questions dabbed his mind continuously, his thought is extremely shaken by the information he got from the Director. He has never heard of anything as powerful and dynamic as the liquid gold. To satisfy his curiosity, he looks up google for more information about the liquid gold as he seeks to verify if all that the Director told him about the liquid gold earlier today.

To his wildest imagination, while pervading through the string of information displayed by google, he finds out that the liquid gold refers to breast milk, bewildered and astonished, he exclaims,

'Jeez... I can't believe this liquid gold is a bogus name for breast milk!'. His face is red, his veins tighten their body across his forehead, he becomes sweaty and restless, he wanders between two point in his light-absconded room, filled to brim with anger, questions and worries, he decides to inform his younger sister: Sarah, Jenny's friend, who is a nurse, about this weird discovery of his. As an investigative journalist, he needed to have this information revealed to the media.

****

Sarah picks up her phone after it rang four times. At the other end, he assumes that she was in the hospital attending to an emergency. 'Hello, Sarah!'. He calmly continues, 'I just found out that the rumor about the utilization of the breast milk to produce diary products is true, can you believe that?' Sarah screams, 'My friend, Jenny, lives in there. She had just reached out to me about an ongoing event in there, asking me for my advice' Sarah adds, 'This is dangerous'.

Sarah's brother had come across the rumors apropos the mother milk network some days back, but he never believed in it until he decided to check it out. There was total silence between Sarah and her brother. At her end, Sarah unhesitatingly hung the phone and tries to reach to Jenny, unfortunately, Jenny's line wasn't going through.

CHAPTER EIGHT

Jenny tilts forward, bending her back, trying to imitate the yoga exercise they have in the Sanatorium every Monday, while she does this, small pints of sweat break off from her tiny skin apertures, the ward's tiled floor glows, laid bare across the stream of sunlight breaking into the room, creating a space for her shadow to watch her as she strives at reviving her sanity.

She remembers all that the yoga instructor had told them about the mental ease that heralds into the mind after a yoga routine. She wipes her cheeks against a small napkin, she strolls to the window edge, nails her fragile elbow to the windowsill and smiles.

The Doctor had told her the previous day that she was getting pregnant very soon; her breastmilk was returning and her stay in the Sanatorium is assured, but Jenny found this extremely strange and confounding. She walks back into the center of the ward, a speck of dust lay on her heels, she is unbothered as the last time she had to wear them was when Jack took her out on a date, her mind is reflective, her shoulders drop like drapes falling into quietness at the epilogue of a movie, 'Jack must be fine!', she whispers in her mind, nothing again will take tears out of her eyes, she promised herself this after her baby died prematurely.

She looks at the porcelain placed upon the table closer to the space where she trudges every time her mind is clobbered by worries. Her friends, Charlotte and Amber, have a schedule with the Doctor this morning, but they had promised to return back to her ward. Prior to this, Jenny had disclosed to Amber the proposed plan of the Doctor to get her pregnant, Amber rushed to inform Charlotte, they both jumped happily, hugging and smiling sheepishly like small girls with candies in their hands.

A small party was organized for her, there was a lot of merrymaking and jubilation, she ate and danced till she forgot that she was not pleased with it, they congratulated her, urging to wear her best gown today, but here she is: hands placed atop each other aching to dial Sarah's number, everything seem dangerous and suspicious, only Sarah can help her out of this catastrophic happening that she foresee.

****

The first dial did not go through, she redials it, her hands her shaky, trembling, furious and slippery to bear the thoughts of her mind, she needs to speak with Sarah; she drops the napkin on her shoulder and redials Sarah's number. Unfortunately, there was no connection in the Sanatorium. She ponders for a while and decides to check outside of the Sanatorium. At this point, she was fearless, she did not care about the rules that guided their movement and activities in the Sanatorium. All she wanted was a discussion with her friend; her trusted friend, Sarah. Meandering through the hallway fearlessly, she stops at the exit of the Sanatorium building, she knows

Charlotte and Amber would be on their way to her ward, she looks back to see if anyone is trailing her, she finds nothing suspicious, not even her shadow.

When she thinks she had eluded perfectly all and sundry, the security men find her stuck at the main gate,

'Who are you?' Jenny asks fidgeting like a petal soaked with stream waters, she shrugs off the fear, and asks again like Sarah had taught to her to do every time fear grips her mind, 'Who are you?'

The first man does not look British, his hair is brown, his tongue ran out in a rush like that of a Russian, he is broad and heavily build, just like Jack, his voice is husky, tangled with rough patches,

'Where are you going to?' The second man sounds like a British, he has a satirical scar on his cheek, and his eyes look like red moon swarming through the vast expanse of a dark sky. Jenny removes her hands embarrassingly from the gate. In a jiffy, they bundle her and drag to the Director's office.

****

'Jenny, you are never allowed to leave the Sanatorium!' the Director peers into her eyes like an angry wolf yelling out to its pack of soldiers, Jenny shivers at every word that spiraled out of his bloodied mouth,

'This is because of your health, Jenny!' the Director pretends to be calm and affectionate, this jolts down the fear in Jenny. He continues, 'You need to get hold of yourself properly before you get yourself involved in several strenuous activities'. Jenny mind is calm, she replies lifelessly like a bird struggling to stay afloat in pool,

'I fully understand, Director'

'The nutrition and stress might affect the pregnancy and the production of milk' the Director retorts, he looks up at her contract file and says,

'Jenny, your time is not over, you still have to stay in this Sanatorium'

CHAPTER NINE

Jenny is slightly bothered; totally confused, she turns around. Instead of going to her ward, she darts to Charlotte and Amber's ward, her gown is dirtied with finger-strips smeared by the long-hefty fingers of those security personnel. Jenny is less bothered about her dress, her lips tamed by the supple tang of drought, there is a loud groan in the lowermost of her belly- she is hungry, but she is undaunted by its ferocious fangs. Unbeknownst to her, there is a little cut on her kneecap, she is unaware until she feels a sharp pain thrust into her bone,

'Ouch…This hurts!' She stops running, her face becomes red, slowly and painfully she arrives at Charlotte and Amber's ward,

'Jenny, is all good with you? You look knackered!' Charlotte's trickles in from the loo.

'She doesn't look fine' Amber adds. She walks over to Jenny and place her palm on her forehead, she feels nothing, only pints of sweats fuming upon Jenny's forehead.

'I am all fine!' Jenny pretends to be fine, but deep down, her heart pants heavily, while Charlotte returns to her cot, Jenny finds a cushion close to the window where finds Charlotte's favorite heels underneath a small table carrying a lampshade, she sits and folds her leg atop each other.

Amber throws a light joke, Charlotte laughs hard, Jenny could not tell how they found this amusing, neither could she tell why they find staying in this Sanatorium gracious but she could tell that they have no regrets and they are utterly unbothered,

'What did you have for breakfast, Jenny?' Amber pulls a gown from the wardrobe, turns around and tells Jenny to try it on. Charlottes suspects Jenny's absentminded-ness and retorts,

'Jenny, what did you have for breakfast?' Jenny looks away from the dress Amber threw at her and bravely asks,

'Have you guys ever left the Sanatorium?' Jenny an-grily continues, while Charlotte and Amber stunningly peer at her,

'Have you guys ever contacted your families and friends since you came into this Sanatorium?' Jenny is furious, she hates that they never cared about leaving the Sanatorium; she hates that they snubbed her every time she asks pertinent questions about the state of the Sanatorium. No one uttered a word after Jenny's rant ended. Out of the blues, Charlotte speaks up crazily, un-fettered,

'Yes, we have families but we do not ever want to see them again!' Her voice is harsh, she doesn't care about who is out there waiting for, she continues, 'They all de-serted me when I needed them the most. They are callous people. I don't ever want to associate with them!' Jenny is moved to tears, Amber retorts, 'We have chosen to find bliss and comfort in the beauty of this Sanatorium. Those persons out there do not care about us. They treated us like pigs when we needed them. They threw our bags out there on the streets like beggars. They told us never to return to them'

Jenny abruptly utters, 'I am sorry for all of this. I am so sorry. I should not have brought this up. It is bitter to know that your families and friends threw you out at the most delicate moment of your lives'

'We have all that we want here. We eat and sleep like birds. We get paid for an inherent ability. What else do we need?' Charlotte confidently asks.

'We have no reason at all to leave this Sanatorium; it is our heaven on earth, Jenny. Take a cursory look at your skin, your dress, isn't this humane?' Amber shows no remorse at all for the choice they have chosen.

Although, Jenny finds sense in what Charlotte and Amber told her earlier, she still isn't satisfied at this fate that has suddenly beclouded the minds of Charlotte and Amber. Nevertheless, she decides to call Sarah, who else can she run to, only Sarah knows her well enough to be able to possess perfectly her emotion. She is determined to contact Sarah and no one in the Sanatorium will stop her from getting through her best friend.

****

Christmas is close, the serenity of the Sanatorium began to take a different direction, huge Christmas trees get planted at every spot in the Sanatorium. Jenny finds this surprising until the biggest of them happened- on her bed sleeping, she hears a knock on her door, when she gets to the door, she finds a small gift, the person already gone with no trace at all. When she gets to Charlotte and Amber's ward, she finds out that everyone in the Sanatorium gets a gift every Christmas eve,

'It is the routine here once it is Christmas eve' Charlotte excitingly reveals. Amidst this riveting aura of bliss, Jenny discovers that there is a group of choristers in the Sanatorium, theatre plays and intriguing concerts. This group of choristers were organized to sing yearly at the Christmas eve in the Sanatorium, during their sonorous rendition, Jenny is moved to tears, she walks up to the Director discreetly and begs for his phone.

'Why do you want my phone?'

'Sir, I need to wish my best friend a merry Christmas!' Jenny retorts pitifully.

First, he disagrees, but she begs insistently, he agrees and leads Jenny into the office. Covertly, he leaves the office without closing the door, he stays mute to one position while he quietly listened to Jenny's conversation over the phone. Jenny gets through to Sarah,

'Hello, Sarah. This is Jenny.' She continues, 'I am still in the Sanatorium. I am pregnant for the second time. I am so happy everything is perfect. I wish you a merry Christmas. Please give a big hug to Alicia.'

Sarah listens to the message, she discovers a mutual slang that only her and Jenny know to mean danger, she becomes troubled and anxious. The first person she decides to reach out for help is her brother.

CHAPTER TEN

Last week at the popular late night show with John Oliver, three nutrition and health experts were invited as guests to the show by the host. They all appeared exuberant to speak about the topic displayed on the T.V Screen. The first guest is Professor Tim Benton, a professor at the University of Leeds; the second guest is Joanna Rowlinson, MD; the third guest is Dr. Steven Murdock.

They were all invited to discuss extensively the healthiness of animal's milk to humans, the appropriateness of consuming animal meats, ways foods are produced, and consumed, thus explaining why waste food is unsustainable from a planetary perspective. John Oliver intelligently engaged these experts about the discussion of animal meat, milk and waste food's unsustainability.

Humans consume animal milk and meats but we are totally ignorant of the cons of this tremendous consumption in our body system. John Oliver threw an intriguing question to Dr. Steven Murdock.

He asked, 'what does humanity stand to gain from the daily consumption of animal milk?'

Dr. Steven Murdock excited to speak, expatiated profoundly, 'Besides humans (and companion animals who are fed by humans), no species drinks milk beyond infancy or drinks the milk of another species. Cow's milk is suited to the nutritional needs of calves, who have four stomachs and gain hundreds of pounds in a matter of months, sometimes weighing more than 1,000 pounds before they are 2 years old.'

He continued, 'Cow's milk is one of the primary causes of food allergies among children. Most people begin to produce less lactase, the enzyme that helps with the digestion of milk, when they are as young as 2 years old. This reduction can lead to lactose intolerance. Millions of American are lactose intolerant, and an estimated 95 percent of Asian-Americans and 80 percent of Native- and African-American suffer from the condition, which can cause bloating, gas, cramps, vomiting, headaches, rashes, and asthma. A U.K. study showed the people who suffered from irregular heartbeats, asthma, headaches, fatigue, and digestive problems showed marked and often complete improvements in their health after cutting milk from their diets.'

John sighed, 'I did not know the human species suffer this much from the consumption of animal milk, especially cows.'

Dr. Steven Murdock retorted, 'Although American women consume tremendous amounts of calcium, their rates of osteoporosis are among the highest in the world. Medical studies indicate that rather than preventing the disease, milk may actually increase women's risk of getting osteoporosis. A Harvard Nurses' Study of more than 77,000 women ages 34 to 59 found that those who consumed two or more glasses of milk per day had higher risks of broken hips and arms than those who drank one glass or less per day. T. Colin Campbell, professor of nutritional biochemistry at Cornell University, said, the association between the intake of animal protein and fracture rates appears to be as strong as that between cigarette smoking and lung cancer. Humans can get all the protein that they need from nuts, seeds, yeast, grains, beans, and other legumes. It is very difficult not to get enough calories from protein when you eat a healthy diet; protein deficiency (also known as 'kwashiorkor') is very rare in the U.S and is usually only a problem for people who live in famine-stricken countries.'

John Oliver nodded affirmatively to all these points substantially outlined by Dr. Steven, he furthered by asking Professor Tim Benton some questions,

'How far has the consumption of animals by human affected global warming?'

Professor Tim Benton snugged and responded, puffed by the knowledge of the looming danger the human species get to attract by this act,

'This is the biggest question of all. Adelaide University's Professor of Climate Change, Barry Brook, estimates that raising animals for human consumption is responsible for half of Australia's short-term global warming gases — that's more than the coal industry.'

He continued, while the other two guests listened without any show of reprobation, 'The Oxford University report describes how avoiding meat and dairy is the 'single biggest way' to reduce your impact on earth. And that's not all. Making the change to a more sustainable plant-based food system will help not only people, it will spare billions of farmed animals from the horrors of factory farms and slaughterhouses, and help save our precious wildlife. Damien Carrington, Environment editor, The Guardian UK, said the new research shows that without meat and dairy consumption, global farmland use could be reduced by more than 75%- an area equivalent to the US, China, European Union and Australia combined – and still feed the world. Loss of wild areas to agriculture is the leading cause of the current mass extinction of wildlife.'

He ended on this note: the way we produce food, consume and waste food is unsustainable from a planetary perspective.

John sighed, clasped his fingers together. Joanna Rowlinson explained that animals, especially, cows need to preserved and nurtured, instead of slaughtering after extracting milk from them. Moved by fear, Joanna Rowlinson expatiated with expertise the need to preserve animals, against the uncontrollable condition of global warming.

At the end of the show: John Oliver together with these three notable guests urged the human species to sustain the world by preserving animals and avoiding the uncontrolled consumption of cow milk; they concluded that letting animals live freely without being hunted is the antidote to the depreciation of global warming.

CHAPTER ELEVEN

Jenny feels a sharp nudge in her lower abdomen, she growls and peers at her stomach longer than normal. It is getting bigger, she said to herself. Elegantly, she places her red, slim, red-nail fingers on her stomach, she thinks about her first child- the child she never had a chance to carry or sing a lullaby for. Contrary to the motherly joy she felt the first time a doctor told her she carried a baby in her womb, she feels disturbed and perturbed by every inch of growth her stomach grows into.

The weather is rigid, sunny and lucid. In the sky, there are clouds breaking into smaller fragments, between the patches of their sail, birds fly across with adorable chirps that leaves the earth beautiful with music. Jenny is not aware about this earthly aesthetic at the moment, rather her mind is the cornerstone of worries hassling for the hook of a decisive moment. Between this tough conduit of weariness, she decides to contact the Director. I need to know the family of the baby in her womb, she mutters to herself.

She darts towards the threshold of the ward, her index finger lugged into her mouth, her mind wanders of the cliff; she thinks about the strange lady who came to visit her in the hospital, who came for the money of the milk for the baby before her pregnancy.

Sarah has been to the Director's office at several delicate moments, this is another delicate moment where she needs to talk to the Director about the throbbing ache in her head. She exits the door into her room, the glint of the iron door against the sun splatters into the pathway as she slams the door. There is a bit of noise in the wards as she sauntered through the pathway, by her right, a lady, unknown, is whispering the lyrics of poetry: this reminds her of Jack; his profound love for poetry and lyricism.

It did not take long before Jenny got to the Director's office. Charlotte and Amber had visited the Director some days back to say 'Hello' to the Director. Jenny did not accompany them. She hates that she was seized and brought to his office the day she needed to speak to her friend, Sarah. She vowed never to see his face again; never to go to his office; never to let his fingers touch her skin.

But now here she is, knocking on his door with a face corrugated with stern wrinkles of frown and discomfort,

'Come in!' The voice is fierce, although comforting like the voice of an unknown preacher down the street of Cornwall.

The door cringes (Sarah opens like an angel seeking the face of its host)

The Director stands to welcome Jenny immediately she entered.

'Welcome, Jenny' He says, reaching out to grab a chair for Jenny.

'Hi, Director'

'Do have your seat, Jenny' He divulges with a crisp smile illuminating his face.

'No. Don't worry, Director. I am fine' She retorts without stuttering for a second.

He is not shocked by Jenny's recalcitrant pose. She has always been this way since she discovered the Sanatorium's secret activities.

'Do you need my help, Jenny?' This time around, his voice is calmer and soothing, enthusiastic to help Jenny with whatever problem she is confronted with.

'Yes. Urhmmm.' She stutters. Thumping her legs to the ground with disappointed.

He retorts in a very tender tone, 'Speak up, Jenny. I really want to help you!'

He got it right this time. His tender-hearted words instilled courage and trust in Jenny, so she spoke.

'Whose family does the baby I breastfed belong to?' she continues, 'I also want to meet the lady that came for the money of the milk for the baby before her pregnancy!'

Immediately after she uttered this voice, the Director helplessly stood up.

'Jenny, these questions are very confidential matters. It is practically impossible for you know the answers behind these questions.' He cajoles her by opening up, he continues, 'Moreover, why do you want to know the answers behind these highly-confidential questions?'

He walks towards Jenny, she draws back trying to ensure that they do not have any body contact, not even the slightest of them.

She tells him that she considers leaving the Sanatorium after she has given birth to the baby; immediately after her lactation has ended, she wants to return to her normal life outside of the Sanatorium.

He informs her that she has the right to leave the Sanatorium at her own will, although, this is only possible as long as she keeps to her contract which she currently has to fulfill before she can be allowed to leave the Sanatorium. He hands out a copy of the contract to Jenny. She takes it without staring at it for a second and return to her room.

When she gets to her room, Jenny drops the copy of the contract on the desk recently placed in her room, and lay silently on her cot without uttering a word.

****

Meanwhile, Sarah tells her brother that Jenny is in big trouble. She begs him to help her contact a lawyer to consider the options to liberate Jenny. Sarah feels bad and cruel. She sobs quietly when no is around; she thinks about Jenny and how she brought all this mayhem upon her innocent friend. She vows to ensure that Jenny get released from the Sanatorium.

CHAPTER TWELVE

Sarah hooks up with her lawyer in a popular canteen down the street of Southampton. She had informed over the phone about Jenny's complication and he had promised vehemently to help her look into it by all possible means. They request for two cups, of hot coffee as the weather seem chilly and wintry. Sarah doesn't wait for the waitress to serve the requested order before she rolled in the wheel for discussion.

Apologetically, she is colorful with guilt and regret for talking her friend, Jenny, into all of this she has found herself in. She avoids peering into the bulgy eyes of the lawyer for so long. Although, he is a friend she had always known right from high school, they have never had to meet outside the framework of formalities; this she so much admire and like.

Abruptly, the lawyer speaks like a bobby interrogating a suspect who has just been arrested for a serious theft case, 'Sarah, I have looked into this case properly, I am deeply sorry to inform you that I see clearly no legal chance of getting Jenny out of the Sanatorium at this moment'

Sarah's mouth is wide-opened, befuddled by the discouraging words of the lawyer, she asks, 'Why do you say so, Lawyer?'

Unhesitatingly, he continues sharply, 'These are the following reasons why it is going to be extremely difficult and impossible to get Jenny out of the Sanatorium!' Sarah's ears are itchy, she needs to know to what are those barricades withdrawing her friend from the embrace of liberty.

'First and foremost, your friend, Jenny, signed a contract agreeing to sell her breastmilk for a fee of five thousand pounds. Also she agreed to become a surrogate mother, by the way, she was paid bountifully for accepting this role. Furthermore, coupled with this staggering and mouth-watering pay, she is also treated and attended to like a queen, bereft of any kind of pressure or intimidation. Finally, there are several medical reasons which prevents her from leaving the Sanatorium at her own will.'

He pauses. Sarah is gloomy and unhappy. She ponders about this whole brouhaha and thumps her legs to the ground. Regretting her decisions, she mutters silently,

'Damn. I push poor Jenny into this, how do I get her out of this mess?'

All of a sudden, Sarah throws a question to the Lawyer, 'Wait. But what about the fact that they sell breast milk to companies that produce mother milk products like cheese or cosmetics?' She continues, 'You could check the website: humanmilk.shop.

'That is great one, Sarah'

The waitress comes along with a tray, carrying two cups of hot coffee. She has an oval face bodied by a cassock that seems bigger than her stature. As she drops the tray on the glass-created table, the lawyer continued,

'I will investigate thoroughly on that. Moreover, it is illegal to carry out such an act, Sarah' He says with a cold face repellant of whatever emotion Sarah was trying to transfer to him by her talks and attitudinal dispositions.

'I sincerely doubt if this will change Jenny's situation for good, Sarah' He folds his arms across his broad chest and grabs his coffee for a terse sip.

'Ermhh...Ermhhh.' He coughs, clearing his throat of any mucus.

'Jenny is like a dairy cow with a contract that guarantees best treatment and a very attractive payment' He adds as he stands up to take his leave.

Sarah looks pensive. She doesn't have a sip of her coffee before dragging her legs behind the lawyer like a child resuming to college, scared of bullies and unknown aliens.

****

In the Sanatorium, Jenny is restless, pacing up and down the whole building, searching for Scarlet and Charlotte who are assiduously preparing for a party. Both of them are about to leave the Sanatorium after spending so much in this place. When Jenny sees them, they say to her happily,

'Our time here is over and we will now fulfill the last part of our contract: That is the party..'

CHAPTER THIRTEEN

No one is inside the ward with Jenny. She is all alone. Only the music of birds chirping seep into the pores of her eardrum. Jenny holds the document tightly. She has been through moments she never thought she would survive. Here she is stuck in her ward. She hums a dirge. Her mind wanders off. She sees Jack again.

She feels a sharp thrust of pain in her heart, she gropes her chest and bend over the table. Silently, she opens the document, she doesn't read aloud, she uses her index finger- red and slender to trace the alphabets arranged intelligently into a contractual statement. It reads: Stay and work until menopause. Afterwards, you are going to donate your organs or you find two women to replace you. Nevertheless, the paid money will go to the Sanatorium in case of death.

Tangible goosebumps grow over her skin immediately she hit a caesura at the end of the document's contractual analysis. Her face goes pale like a withered leave trolled by a ferocious wind. She looks up at her face in the mirror hung by the shoe-stack, her bones hassle with movement, she remains immovable- an abandoned item stuck in the ditch.

She had decided some days back she was never spilling anything to Charlotte and Amber, although, Sarah knows everything, even to the minute details of what food she has for breakfast, lunch and dinner. She ponders about telling them all that has become her fate since she approached the Director.

'Sarah isn't here!' She mutters to herself. The light-bulb clings over her head. A supple part of reminisce hits her introspective abode. 'I will give it a trial. I am going to talk to Charlotte and Amber' She gives herself a nudge. 'Yes, I got this!' She whispers aloud affirmatively.

****

After narrating the whole scenario to Charlotte and Amber, Jenny gives a fake smile between the wrinkles of disgust on her face. They find nothing bad about the content of the document.

'What are you worried about, Jenny?' Amber is the first to utter a statement.

'Heaven. This is glorious and exciting!' Charlotte continues, 'I feel this is the best thing that will ever come your way, girl! Grab it. Take it. Do not be repulsive towards this.'

The Sanatorium offers everything a woman dreams of and they finally lived the perfect life they so much desire like a harlot desiring the caress of a man. Charlotte and Amber calls the life they enjoy in the Sanatorium a life of luxury; a life protected from all the trouble and problems other women encounter every day of their lives.

'This is the best thing to have happened to me!' Amber grabs Jenny by her slender shoulders. Charlotte thinks esoterically while Amber talks to Jenny like a mother talks to her only daughter.

'After having to enjoy such a beautiful life in here, you are presented the opportunity to donate your organs and pass away peacefully before our bodies become old, ugly and punished by gruesome symptoms. Jenny, here it is: the perfect life! The best way to be human in a society that is inhumane' Amber concludes.

Jenny shrugs off this talks from Charlotte and Amber. She returns to her ward quietly like a snail moisturized by rain and mud.

****

Immediately after the party in the evening, they say goodbye to everyone. In a jiffy, a Bentley Limousine drives in to ferry them to another place. Jenny delivers her baby that night due to psychological stress. The doctors are kind and compassionate. Everyone in the Sanatorium is unusually kind and affectionate. The doctors urge Jenny to relax and keep a sane mind. They inform her that her body is fine. They inform her she can have another insemination in two weeks.

CHAPTER FOURTEEN

Jenny is against having another insemination; she doesn't want another treatment. Although, she desires to leave the Sanatorium this very moment. The Director soothes Jenny's troubled mind; he talks in a comely and affectionate manner that endears him to her as she listens quietly to the words he has to tell her.

'Jenny, I want you to listen and pay attention to all that I want to say to you.'

(Jenny scoffs) 'Great. I will love to hear that.'

The Director begins to unfold series of events to her. He tells her how the Sanatorium came into existence, the Sanatorium's operative dynamism; the milk collected reveals what they are used for. He makes a promise to Jenny. He promised that he would get her in contact with Sarah, the nurse, Jenny's best friend, who brought her into the Sanatorium.

He also tells Jenny about the Sanatorium's goal: giving hopes to desperate women, availing a life full of luxury to them. He continues,

'Jenny, in return for this immense kindness that we offer, these women, like you, produce milk that is sold to the industry for the production of breast milk products like butter, yogurt, cheese, and cosmetics. These products are distributed to privileged customers who appreciate the benefit of human milk products. He reveals to her that they are covertly called HMP (Human Milk Producers). He explains to her that this how they name them internally.

Jenny folds her arms across her chest, draws closer to him, oblivious of the stream of sweat sliding down her smooth chin.

He calls her forth again like he was about to have her follow him to a hideout, 'Jenny, do not expect a good life outside of this Sanatorium. These women you find here agree to donate their organs after menopause to ensure that they end their life with dignity.'

Jenny trembles, her innards twisted by surprise; she calls the whole scenario crazy and insane. The shock she gets from this information is almost the same as the one she suffered from when she heard the news of Jack's demise.

The Director calmly asks if she has ever consumed dairy products. She says, Yes. Nodding affirmatively to the question posed to her by the Director. The Director tells her that this is precisely the same, just with human females.

He says if humans can treat animals the same way: get milk from them and later kill them, there is nothing wrong with how the Sanatorium treats these human females. Moreover, these women are not eventually killed like those animals. Instead, they give out their body organs when they hit menopause.

****

Finally, he tells her that Sarah will come and pick her up to explain how she can find two women to replace her; this is to ensure that she fulfills her part of the contract; thus, she can leave the Sanatorium forever together with the money, which has summed up to over 150,000 pounds. The Director tells her that she has just barely four weeks to find someone to replace her in the Sanatorium.

On the other end, Sarah knows what to do because she lured Jenny into the Sanatorium as the perfect replacement for herself. Jenny is shocked and perplexed about what to think of her dear friend, Sarah.

'Why would Sarah do this to me?' she mutters silently to herself like a nightingale.

CHAPTER FIFTEEN

The city's supple breeze stays elevated within the chromosome of chilliness and serenity. Jenny finds Sarah after a long ache throbbed in her heart concerning Sarah's involvement and knowing in luring her to the Sanatorium.

'Sarah, why did you do this?'

Sarah is speechless. There are one thousand and ten things recycling in Sarah's head and she is clueless.

'What might be wrong, Jenny?' Sarah is soft-hearted; her speeches are laced with tenderness and smoothness. Her eyes loop inside their frames, peering out innocently like the eyes of a deer, ambushed by lions.

Jenny divulges all that she heard to Sarah. Tears stroll down her eyes as she opens up to her. Beside the ache of being lured into Sanatorium, she feels so much betrayal finding out that Sarah was a major influence in the play out of the whole event.

Sarah is apologetic. She holds Jenny's arms, her face downtrodden and pallid, she says,

'I was a drug addict, Jenny'

The rustling of tulips, the squeaks of birds stretching the sky, the tingling soar of clouds in the foamy mouth of the heavens and the patches of brilliance evidence in the environment.

Jenny raises her brows in awe of what just ran out of Sarah's mouth, Sarah continues,

'I got pregnant many times but I lost the babies before birth'

'Wow!' Jenny's mouth takes a round shape as she found Sarah's revelation flabbergasting and interesting.

'One day, I offered to have a special therapy in order to save to my life. So I came to the Sanatorium and stayed there for five years.'

'Wow!' At this point, Jenny begins to quiver, unable to withstand the momentum of all that she is listening to.

'I give birth to three babies while I stayed at the Sanatorium before I asked to be released'

'Three babies, Sarah?'

'Yes!'

'You never mentioned any of this to me!'

'I know. I am sorry, Jenny'

'When I requested to leave, I was told to recommend two women to replace, so I recommended you as one of the women.'

Jenny opens her eyes wide.

'The second woman I recommended was a nineteen-year-old girl that wanted to run away from her because she was carrying her father's baby.'

Jenny begins to understand Sarah's dilemma as at the time she was in the Sanatorium she needed to recommend two women to be let go.

'Jenny, I am really sorry for all I got you into'

Jenny understands that Sarah might be her only chance. In her mind, she relates keenly with Sarah's narration, thus she feels that Sarah is really sorry for all that has happened. She holds Sarah tightly. Affectionately bounded by love, they share a warm and sincere hug.

****

Jenny starts working as a nurse at the women's clinic where she met Sarah. Her world seems to be falling within the grip of her control and she likes it, extremely. While she works as nurse at the women's clinic, she is utterly ambivalent as regards the search for a 'replacement womb' until she comes across a seventeen-year-old suicidal girl who killed her own baby after having given birth to the child in the home's bathroom.

CHAPTER SIXTEEN

Jenny is heavily disturbed by Sarah's revelation. Her mind is not at rest. Ever since she met Sarah, she had denounced whatsoever would lure into being vile. She regrets that she never gave Sarah a minute to explain herself before hastily concluding that her best friend is evil.

Nothing is lovelier than having a friend who will go all the way to have your back even in your absence: the calendar atop her jewelry box says this. Jenny thinks about the girl Sarah mentioned earlier. She decides to reach out to her while she scribbled down on a paper safe places where she could hide the girl from her dangerous father. Her mind is stuck in different locations; she pervades through the thick and thin of her head, searching for a place that will be quite safe for this girl, a place her father will never find.

She remembers that the girl carries a child that belongs to her biological father. It is difficult to survive when everyone finds out that the child you nurse belongs to your father- incest is such disgust in society. Jenny thinks of places that will save this young girl from the bully of persons who would hurl insults at her for having a child that belongs to her father. Immediately, the Sanatorium wheels into Jenny's troubled mind.

'I think the Sanatorium is the best place for her!' Jenny thinks out loud, pouring herself a velvety and strawberry wine given to her at the Sanatorium.

'Is she going to succumb to this request?' Jenny considers the poor girl's situation, although she feels her help to move the girl to the Sanatorium will be met with a stern rebuttal from the girl. She gathers herself out of the cushion and hums along to the music playing out of the stereo.

Fortunately, the girl agrees to move to the Sanatorium. 'Do you want to hide from your ruthless father?' Jenny peers into the girl's pale eyes. A spell of silence thrust into her voice; the girl musters the courage to speak, 'Yes!'

'I will move you to a Sanatorium. Your baby will be fine. You will be taken care of properly and paid hugely' The girl is glad. She jumps upon Jenny and tightens her arms around Jenny's waist, gasping heavily. Jenny brings the other woman along with the girl to the Sanatorium.

****

A week after moving two women to the Sanatorium, Jenny finds a pregnant refugee girl of twenty-two years; she does not speak English. The girl was brought into the hospital some days back, laden with bruises and horrible symptoms due to forceful penetration- rape. She bled heavily and was quickly attended to by an emergency operation. Unfortunately, she lost her baby. Jenny walks up to her while she sobs quietly on her bed.

'I love you. I want to help you. I want to give you a new life' The girl looks up in awe of who was speaking;

she understands what Jenny said, although she cannot give a response in English; instead, she nods at every word Jenny said.

After a long discussion where the young girl kept quiet at almost every word Jenny said, she decides to follow Jenny to the Sanatorium. Now Jenny is free to leave the Sanatorium. She already replaced herself with these women.

Jenny is not satisfied to leave the Sanatorium without inquiring about the whereabout of her baby. So she walks up to the Director elegantly, feeling deservedly of honest and straight response,

'Hi, Director!'

'Hey, Jenny. Good, you are free to leave the Sanatorium now.'

'Yes, it is such a beautiful feeling.'

'I want to get all the money I have earned, Director.'

'Oh. That will be fixed.'

'My baby. Yes. I almost forgot. Can I know the family that took my baby in?'

Immediately, the Director's face becomes stern and red. His frown is scary and obvious. His voice is sharp as he replies to Jenny's question,

'You better stop asking questions and move on with your life!' Jenny is fearful. She staggers and waits, pulsating.

CHAPTER SEVENTEEN

Jenny couldn't stay mundane with the distressing thoughts of her unknown child living at the beckon of a different family. She moves to Sarah's apartment. In dire need of a private apartment and job, she grieves the unavailability of all these necessities.

Most times, alone at home, she rehearses some weird dance moves she had seen on the television; Jenny sings for two minutes, host herself to mouthwatering cuisines, then she sleeps off throbbing her index finger over her chest, undoing the silence of the whirlwind spooling over the house roof, thinking about her child like a dying mother.

Beyond the blindfolding angst of living without knowing her child's whereabouts, she is also perturbed about getting the girls out of the Sanatorium. She mutters to herself angrily. She remembers the Director's words the last time she visited the Sanatorium. Everything he had said spites her.

'I am going to help these girls get out of the Sanatorium.' She says to herself. She is clueless about how to go about it, but she is sure that Sarah can help around this and make it possible. She feels excited, ready to enact all strength to see those girls gain freedom again.

She decides to talk to Sarah about this when Sarah comes around.

****

Sarah doesn't hide her love for Jenny. She loves Jenny so much that saying no to Jenny's request seem like a mountain rooted to the depth of an ocean- impossible to reject or overturn. Jenny talks to Sarah about all she had thought about earlier in the afternoon,

'Sarah, help me save those girls from the Sanatorium.'

'OK' She drags her feet tiredly to the other end of the room, using her hands to unbutton her sleeve, exposing her spotless skin,

'I will take you to the Lawyer' Sarah concludes.

The Lawyer is calm and reserved. His gait is comely and refined. Sarah's brother is around, too. He is wearing a faded face-cap, his brawls are firm, his face carries a moribund look, he is calm, enchanted by the Lawyer's conspicuous expertise.

After several bouts of discussion, the Lawyer informs Jenny that every step to be channeled towards the release of those girls must be legally corroborated.

'What is the replacement strategy going to be like then, Lawyer?

'This is a normal business manner, Jenny, ' The Lawyer retorts in a way that cremates Jenny's mind with a solidified confidence.

He furthers, 'Apropos the donated organs, there is much to prove!'

****

Unable to take the contract with her, coupled with her failure to reach out to the girls, Jenny is downtrodden and sad. Guilt embraces her in all manner of intimacy. She feels unwell for sending the girls to the Sanatorium with no obvious way of getting them out of the Sanatorium. She keeps to herself like an injured bird. This has to be one of the worst moments of her life.

'I should not have sent the girls to the Sanatorium.' She hates herself for doing this at the expense of ensuring that there are alternatives to get them out of the Sanatorium.

CHAPTER EIGHTEEN

After so much search for a job, Jenny finds one, she starts working as a housemaid for a Russian Media Mogul who resides in London. Everything she has come to enjoy in life is a result of grace.

Many times, she finds her totally speechless, unable to fathom the reason why she has enjoyed so much kindness from persons she does not know- she remembers Jacks, Sarah and Charlotte. This Russian Media Mogul treats Jenny well. Jenny thinks about how she got this job and laugh really hard at how much she had despised applying.

Thanks to Sarah for pushing her towards applying for the job. She is offered different nutritious recipes to eat at all times. Jenny is treated in a comely and friendly manner.

Since she began working, the Russia Media Mogul has never yelled at her, she has never had to weep countlessly because of the treatment she received here. Her life has turned into a fresh page, inked by amazing and benign memories, inspired by the kindness and care she receives from her boss.

****

Her nightmares begin to fade away like footmarks swept away by the ripples of a sea-water. She slowly begins to forget the Sanatorium trauma, hinging on to the new memories of love she finds from working with this Russian Media Mogul.

In her sleep, she still suffers a stern thrust of nightmares beclouded by the memories of her time in the Sanatorium. With time, she finds herself embracing the newness of her new life, letting go of the unwholesome thoughts of her past life in the Sanatorium.

Her life begins to recoil into normalcy, devoid of the thought of the two girls she took to the Sanatorium to replace her. Jenny feels renewed and refreshed, enwrapped by the icing of her new life, her new boss, and her new job.

Most times, she sits in the verandah, sipping a hot cup of coffee, listening to the rustlings of the trees, the yearnings of the birds winging, the silence of her red-colored toes, and the blankness of the cloud, enfolding her brawls across sunlight.

CHAPTER NINETEEN

It is the last day of the month. The city is busy with flamboyant cars taking itches from the swift glance of Jenny from the house's ballroom. She decides to keep herself busy. Many times, after the completion of a task, she takes a nap, stretch by the window and inhale the mint slowly. She strolls towards the bathroom, peers into the bathtub, an awful smell oozes out, making her flinch back two inches while trying to get a scrub and towel to clean it.

She turns on the bathroom's tap. Holds and folds the curtain's drapes. Her hand reddens with double-line veins muscling the halo of sunlight from a distant sky-stare. Between this bout of activities, Jenny finds human-milk cosmetics in the bathroom- her boss' wife's bathroom, while cleaning the bathtub. She takes and hide it under her gown.

Jenny requests for an appointment so as to tell the story of her experience in the Sanatorium. During this appointment, Jenny narrates the entirety of her life in the Sanitarium in a short and affectionate manner. She tells how she was able to escape while replacing herself with two other women. She had decided to inform her boss about all this since they never knew the source of the human-milk cosmetic she had found in her boss' wife's bathroom.

While she weeps, the Russian Mogul takes her hands and fix his gaze heavily upon her, 'I will see what I can do to help you, Jenny'. Jenny does not believe what he is saying; she is shocked, elevated to haziness by this profound affection by her Russian boss. Nevertheless, he does not make her too hopeful. She explains, 'Human milk are breastmilk extracted from women who lived in the Sanatorium. This milk is refined and sold as component of very good and healthy product that people consume daily. These products are capable of curing terminal diseases, strengthening the muscles, and increasing one's lifespan.'

'Human milk gotten from mothers are like dairy products extracted from cows' he retorts. Cows are not treated fair and good despite being the source of many dairy products, the Russian boss opines. It is unfair that these animals that produce components used to make products that are of immense advantage to humanity are treated in bestial ways.

There should be a fair, healthy, and respectful ways to treat dairy cows, sheep, or animals that provide humanity with eggs and meats, Jenny utters. Some of these animals are treated fairly by some persons, if animals can be treated healthily, why not do the same for women who give out breastmilk that become vital components of a plethora of healthy products? He asks.

If we must retain our humanness, we must learn to treat dairy cows, sheep, and animals fairly. Although many take little cognizance of how they treat these animals, instead their focus is hinged upon continuous consumption, he concludes.

While the discussion ensued, he doesn't give Jenny any hope of seeming capable and willing to get the two ladies out, instead he assures Jenny that he would instruct his secretary to make an appointment with the Director.

CHAPTER TWENTY

Silently he glides through the doorway down to the threshold of the Director's office. The Russian Business Mogul had planned to pay an unprecedented visit to the Sanatorium. He looks around, picking a powerful beam of suspicion. A lady walks up to ask why he was present in the Sanatorium. He explains things to her in a manner that seems like he was wooing a lady.

The lady shows him the way to the Director's office; in his mind, a hearty outburst seized his thoughts. Two knocks at the door, the Director tells the stranger- the Russian Business Mogul to come. After a brief pretentious discussion with the Director. They agree to inspect the Sanatorium as he had feigned to be an investor to the Director.

They stop first at the neatly arranged wards. The Russian glance through them and find them fanciful, 'this is such an amazing lineup.' The Director swells with a smirk and retorts, 'Yes. That is the good work we do hear, sir'. They take few steps forward and stop at a spot.

The Russian notices how well the MPE milk-producing employees are treated. He feels a stern urge to inquire from the Director more about the MPEs. The Director gladly tells him everything about it. Like an actor, he pretends to be highly satisfied, pompous, and exuberant; he wittingly slips a question into the earlobe of the Director.

'Can I buy two of the MPEs to start my farm?' The Director stares at him in dismay. He rejects. 'Sir, you cannot buy two of the MPEs!'. The Russian Mogul is silently surprised by this refusal. 'Why can't I get them?' He asks. 'Sir, you can only invest in the recycling of biological waste.'

'Hmmm...Why do you say so?' He is perplexed by this offer thrown to him by the Director. Before the Director could think of any reply, he added, 'I do not understand your reason for declining my request to purchase two of the MPEs to start my farm.'

The Director chooses to answer calmly, having noticed that the Russian Mogul knew nothing about the modus operandi of the Sanatorium. 'You know how nature works. Pregnancies cause biological waste. We have a good market for that also, sir.'

The Russian Mogul bites his lips hard as the Director spoke like a priest before a cathedral pew filled with sinners. He tries to hide the shock on his face, but it was practically impossible to do that. He looks at the Director unfettered by the angst brimming in the lower-edges of his eyes.

At that moment, he realized that the Director was referring to the newborn babies who are taken from their mothers instantly at birth. He holds his shirt tightly, pretending to be delighted about the news from the Director.

This was the moment when he realized that the story was just about to begin …

Zeitfracht Medien GmbH
Ferdinand-Jühlke-Straße 7
99095 Erfurt, Deutschland
produktsicherheit@kolibri360.de